Tips for Reading Together

Children learn best when reading is fun.

- Talk about the title and the pictures on the cover.
- Look through the pictures together and discuss what you think the story might be about.
- Read the story together, inviting your child to read with you.
- Give lots of praise as your child reads with you, and help them when necessary.
- Try different ways of helping if they get stuck on a word. For example: refer to the picture, or read the first sound or syllable of the word, or read the whole sentence. Focus on the meaning.
- Have fun finding the hidden minibeasts.
- Re-read the story later, encouraging your child to read as much of it as they can.

Children enjoy re-reading stories and this helps to build their confidence.

Have fun!

Find these 10 different minibeasts hidden in the pictures.

The Old Tree Stump

Roderick Hunt • Alex Brychta

OXFORD
UNIVERSITY PRESS

"That old stump has to go,"
said Dad.

Dad pulled the old stump,
but it didn't come up.

Dad called Mum to help.
"I'll push it. You pull it,"
said Dad.

"When I say pull," said Dad,
"I want you to pull!"

Mum pulled and pulled, but
the stump didn't come up.

Dad called Biff.

"I want you to pull," said Dad.

Mum and Biff pulled...

but the stump still didn't come up.

Dad wanted Chip to help.

"When I shout pull," said Dad,

"I want you to pull."

They all pulled...
but the stump still didn't come up.

Kipper wanted to help.

"Come on, then," said Dad.

"When I shout pull... PULL!"

They pulled and they pulled…
but the stump still didn't come up.

"I'll pull as well," said Dad.

"When I yell pull... PULL!"

They all pulled and pulled...
but the stump still didn't come up.

Floppy saw a bone.

He dug and he dug, and…

up came the stump!

BUMP!

"Good old Floppy!" said Chip.

Think about the story

How did the stump come up in the end?

Which part of the story did you find the funniest?

Have you ever read the Enormous Turnip? How is it like this story?

What jobs do you help with at home?

Rhyming odd one out

Which things don't rhyme with snail?

More books for you to enjoy

Read at Home — Funny Fish
Cynthia Rider • Alex Brychta

Read at Home — Poor Old Rabbit!
Cynthia Rider • Alex Brychta

Read at Home — The Old Tree Stump
Roderick Hunt • Alex Brychta

Read at Home — Looking After Gran
Roderick Hunt • Alex Brychta

Read at Home — Silly Races
Roderick Hunt • Alex Brychta

Read at Home — I Can Trick a Tiger
Cynthia Rider • Alex Brychta

Read at Home — The Real Floppy
Roderick Hunt • Alex Brychta

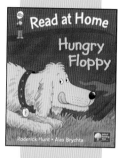

Read at Home — Hungry Floppy
Roderick Hunt • Alex Brychta

Read at Home — Dad's Birthday
Cynthia Rider • Alex Brychta

Read at Home — Floppy and the Bone
Cynthia Rider • Alex Brychta

Read at Home — The Spaceship
Roderick Hunt • Alex Brychta

Read at Home — Husky Adventure
Roderick Hunt • Alex Brychta

Level 1: Getting Ready

Level 2: Starting to Read

Level 3: Becoming a Reader

Level 4: Building Confidence

OXFORD
UNIVERSITY PRESS

Great Clarendon Street,
Oxford OX2 6DP

Text © Roderick Hunt
Illustrations © Alex Brychta 2005
Designed by Andy Wilson

First published 2005

ISBN 0 19 838560 9

10 9 8 7 6 5 4 3 2

Printed in China by Imago

Read at Home — Handbook — Helping Your Child to Read
Kate Ruttle and Annemarie Young